Peppa Pig™

School Bus Trip

Peppa and her friends are going on a school bus trip. "Let's check you are all here," says Madame Gazelle. "Here!" cries Peppa.

Woof!

Baaa! Grunt! Snort!

"Today," begins Madame Gazelle, "we are going on a trip to the mountains!"

"Hooray!"
cheer all the children.

Peppa and Suzy are already a little hungry. "Please can we eat our lunch now?" they ask Madame Gazelle.

"Why not eat your apples and save the rest for the picnic?" she replies. Crunch! Crunch!

The bus has arrived at the foot of the mountain. The road is very steep! "Come on bus! You can make it!" everyone cheers.

Peppa and her friends have finally made it to the top of the mountain.

"Look at the view!"
gasps Madame Gazelle.
All the children look out
over the valley.

"Wow!" sighs Peppa, loudly.
"Wow! Wow! Wow!" Peppa hears
in the distance.
"What was that?" she asks quietly.
"It's your echo, Peppa!"
replies Madame Gazelle.

"An echo is the sound you hear when you speak loudly in the mountains," explains Madame Gazelle.
Grunt! Woof! Baaa! Snort!

Now it's time for a picnic lunch. Peppa loves picnics. Everyone loves picnics! Munch! Slurp! Munch! Yum! Yum!

"Where are the ducks?" asks Peppa, taking a bite of her sandwich. "They always turn up when we have picnics."

Quack! Quack! Quack!
Here come the ducks.
"Hello! Would you like some bread?"
Peppa asks them. The ducks are very
lucky today. There is plenty of bread!